D1499725

Finley Flowers

Pet-rified

BY JESSICA YOUNG
ILLUSTRATED BY JESSICA SECHERET

PICTURE WINDOW BOOKS
a capstone imprint

Finley Flowers is published by Picture Window Books
a Capstone imprint
1710 Roe Crest Drive
North Mankato, MN 56001
www.mycapstone.com

Library of Congress Cataloging-in-Publication Data is available
on the Library of Congress website.

ISBN: 978-1-4795-9805-2 (library hardcover)
ISBN: 978-1-4795-9809-0 (paper over board)
ISBN: 978-1-4795-9825-0 (eBook PDF)
ISBN: 978-1-4795-9829-8 (reflowable epub)

Summary: Finley takes on a pet-sitting job in an effort to convince her parents she should have a pet of her own. But her neighbor's cat turns out to be more trouble than anticipated.

Editor: Alison Deering
Designer: Lori Bye

Vector Images: Shutterstock ©

Printed and bound in the USA.
010400F17

For Ali and everyone on Finley's Fin-tastic team

TABLE OF CONTENTS

Chapter 1
PICK A PET

Finley Flowers plunked her backpack down on the kitchen table and rifled through it. "Has anyone seen my lucky rock? I put it in here so I'd have it for my geography test this morning, but when I got to school it was gone."

Finley's older brother, Zack, looked up from his homework. "You don't need a lucky rock for a test. You just need to study." He held up his math book. "Which is what I'm trying to do right now. Anyway, there's no such thing as a lucky rock."

"For your information, I did study," Finley said, dumping out the rest of her backpack. "And there is too such a thing as a lucky rock — I have one."

Zack smirked. "What's so lucky about it?"

"It's smooth and gray with little white flecks. And it fits just right in my hand."

Zack raised an eyebrow. "So what makes it *lucky*?"

Finley shrugged. "I don't know — magic? I just want to know if you've seen it."

"Nope," Zack said. "But there are tons of rocks in the driveway. Why don't you get one of those?"

Finley sighed. "That's just gravel."

"Maybe it's *magic* gravel," Zack said. Then he burst out laughing.

Finley glared at her brother, and he ducked behind his book. Just then, their little sister, Evie, bounded into the kitchen and grabbed an apple from the bowl on the table.

"My lucky rock is missing," Finley told her. "Have you seen it?"

Evie chomped on her apple. "What does it look like?"

"It's smooth and gray. About as big as a strawberry but flatter."

"I found a rock kind of like that this morning on the porch," Evie said.

Finley's eyes lit up. "It must have fallen out of my backpack. Where is it?"

"I didn't know it was yours. I took it to school to show Ms. Patel."

Finley rolled her eyes. "Well, I need it back."

"I wish I could give it back." Evie looked at her feet. "But I lost it."

"You *lost* it?"

"I'll find you another one," Evie offered.

"You can't," Finley said glumly. "I got it at the beach when we went to visit Grandma." She heaved her backpack onto her shoulder and plodded upstairs to do her homework.

Zack and Evie never understand, she thought. *Sometimes having siblings is harder than a geography test.*

* * *

The next morning, Finley caught up with her friends Henry, Olivia, and Kate on the way to class.

"Did you hear that Lia got a new puppy?" Henry said, hanging up his jacket.

"Lia said her mom might bring it to school sometime," Kate added. "She got it to keep Lia company since her older brother is always busy now that he's in high school."

Finley tugged her jacket off and hung it in her cubby. "I wish I could trade Zack and Evie for a pet. Pets don't laugh at you and act like they know everything. And they don't take your stuff and lose it."

"The best part about pets is that they accept you the way you are," Olivia said. "Like my chinchilla, Camilla — she doesn't care if I've brushed my hair or what grade I got on a test — she's just glad to see me."

"Same with our old dog, Winnie," Henry said. "She was always on my team no matter what."

Finley sighed. "I've always wanted a pet, but my parents think it's too much work. Mom says she can't take care of another living thing. We don't even have any indoor plants."

"But *you'd* take care of it," Olivia said as they walked into class. "What would she say to that?"

Finley shrugged. "I don't know. I guess it couldn't hurt to ask."

"We should make you a pet wish list first," Henry said, setting his books on his desk. "That way, you can narrow it down before you ask them." He opened his notebook and grabbed a pencil. "Okay — pick a pet."

Finley smiled dreamily. "If I could get any pet, I'd get a llama."

"A *llama*?" Henry and Olivia said together.

Finley nodded. "They have graceful necks and long eyelashes, and they're covered in wool I could knit with. Plus, it could carry my backpack — I'd even ride it to school!"

"You could park it by the bike rack," Henry suggested. "Llamas are cool. They're supposed to be really smart. And they hum — I saw it on a nature show."

"Why do they hum?" Olivia asked.

"Because they don't know the words." Henry grinned. "Actually, the moms hum to communicate with their babies."

"Llama lullabies," Finley said. "Another reason to love them."

"What about something a bit smaller?" Olivia suggested. "Like a lizard — or a hamster?"

Finley shook her head. "Mom's not crazy about rodents. And Dad's scared of lizards."

"Even a cute little one, like a gecko?" Olivia said. "Some of them are as small as a dime."

Finley nodded. "When Dad was a kid, my aunt Grace told him that lizards were baby dinosaurs, and he never got over it."

"That makes sense," Henry said. "The word *dinosaur* actually means fearfully great lizard."

"How do you know that?" Finley asked.

"I was crazy about dinosaurs in preschool," Henry said. "I read a ton of dinosaur books. Triceratops was my favorite — that's what *I* always wanted for a pet."

"What about a puppy?" Olivia suggested.

Finley nodded. "I'd love a puppy. Or a miniature pony. Or a parrot I could train to speak French. But a llama is definitely my first choice."

Henry finished writing the list and circled the word *llama*. Then he ripped the page out of his notebook and handed it to Finley.

"There you go," he said, just as their teacher, Ms. Bird, announced it was time to line up for library.

Finley shoved the list into her pocket. She tried not to let her hopes bubble up, but as the class filed down the hall, she couldn't help pulling the paper out to sneak a peek.

When they arrived at the library, Finley immediately checked out some books on pets. If she was going to convince her parents, she needed to do her research.

Mom and Dad love facts, she thought, leafing through the books and taking notes in her sketchbook. *And if I'm going to convince them to get a pet, I'm going to need lots to back me up. I'll be so prepared there's no way they can say no!*

Chapter 2
LLAMA DRAMA

That night at dinner, Evie gave the family a lesson on volcanoes, and Zack summed up his math test. Finley sprinkled cheese on her spaghetti and ate, waiting for her turn to talk.

Finally, when Zack had finished, Mom turned to Finley. "What about you?" she asked. "What have you been up to?"

"Well . . ." Finley said slowly, "I've been thinking."

Dad twirled his spaghetti. "What's growing in your idea garden?"

Finley took a deep breath. "I know I've asked about having a pet before," she began, "but I'm older now, and I'm really ready." She took out her sketchbook to make sure she covered her main points. "I did some research. There are lots of great reasons to have a pet. They can even make you healthier."

Dad raised his eyebrows. "Really?"

Finley nodded. "And I know you want us to be healthy."

Mom smiled. "Just because pets can make people healthier doesn't mean you'll get sick if you don't have one."

Finley clasped her hands together and made a pitiful face. "I'm already sick," she said. "Sick with longing." Then she turned to Dad. "Also, I've noticed you've both been a little stressed lately."

Mom looked surprised. “We have?”

Finley nodded. “Pets lower stress levels too.”

“Amazing.” Dad smiled.

"You're very persuasive," Mom said. "One day when you get your own place, you can have all the pets you want."

"Better start saving," Zack warned. "Pet food, cat litter, vet bills . . ."

Finley glared at her brother. "Don't worry," she said. "I'll make sure I can take care of them. Besides, all they really need is love."

"And food," Zack said, "and water, and shots . . ."

"Just curious," Mom said, "what type of pet did you have in mind?"

Finley handed Mom the list.

Mom put her fork down and read. "A llama?"

"A llama!" Zack doubled over, laughing.

Evie clapped her hands together. "Llamas are so cute! I love the way they chew!"

Finley scowled at Zack. "A llama is very practical. We could harvest her wool to knit hats and mittens and sell them to make money to buy her food. Or she could just eat grass and save us the trouble of mowing the lawn."

Mom handed the paper back. "You've really put some thought into this," she said. "But I'm sorry. We just can't have a pet right now. Especially a llama."

Zack launched into another laughing fit.

Finley's stomach sank. Suddenly, she'd lost her appetite. She stood up, crumpled up the list, and threw it in the trash.

It's pointless, she thought. *I'm petless.*

She stomped upstairs to her room and took out her homework. As she was starting her first social studies question, the door opened a crack. Zack poked his head in.

"I'm sorry I made fun of you," he said.

"Don't worry about it," Finley snapped. "I'm used to it."

Zack slipped into her room. "Look, I know you want a pet — I wouldn't mind having one too. But a *llama*? Why?"

Finley shrugged. “Why not?”

“First of all, we’d need to move,” Zack said. “We’d have to get a farm.”

“No, we wouldn’t. It could sleep in my room and graze in the backyard.”

“You couldn’t keep it inside,” Zack said. “Llamas are outdoor animals. And I’m pretty sure it’s illegal to own one in the city.”

Finley sighed. “Why are you always trying to shoot down my ideas?”

“I’m not trying to shoot them down,” Zack said. “They kind of fall down all on their own. Anyway, I’m sorry if I caused any llama drama.”

Finley glared at Zack and pointed to the door. “You are *not* helping.”

“All right, all right,” Zack said, backing out into the hall.

I've got plenty of great ideas, Finley thought, staring at her social studies book. *It's just that nobody appreciates them. One day I'll have a whole houseful of pets, and I'll charge Zack admission just to see them.*

Chapter 3
PURR-FECT PLAN

The next morning, Olivia and Henry were waiting for Finley at the cubbies. "I knew it," Olivia said when she saw Finley's frown. "You should have gone for a puppy."

"You can't go wrong with a dog," Henry said. "They're always happy to see you, and they love you no matter what."

Finley sighed. "Mom says they need too much time and attention."

"What about a cat then?" Henry suggested. "They're not dogs, but they're still cuddly."

"That's a good idea," Olivia agreed. "They don't need walking or training, and they're really independent. Sometimes I think my cat, Coco, doesn't even notice if we're around."

"True," Finley said. "I might have a better chance with a cat."

"The ancient Egyptians believed cats were magical and brought good luck," Henry said. "Cats were treated like royalty. Their owners dressed them in jewels and gave them special treats. Some were even mummified when they died and buried in the *cat*-acombs."

Olivia made a face. "Yuck. Enough with the cat-mummies. Got any other random cat facts?"

Henry nodded. "They're great hunters," he continued. "They can hear better than humans and see better than us in dim light."

"Wow," Finley said. "Cats are pretty cool."

"That reminds me," Olivia said, digging in her backpack, "I brought this to show you." She handed Finley a copy of a magazine with a basketful of kittens on the front.

"What's that — a *cat*-alog?" Henry grinned.

"Ha," Finley said. "Nice one."

"It's *Pet Perfect* magazine," Olivia said. "This month's issue is all about cats."

"Thanks!" Finley said. "Can I keep it over the weekend? I'll bring it to school on Monday."

"You can have it," Olivia told her. "I've got lots of them."

Finley leafed through the magazine. There were kittens lined up on logs and kittens looking at mirrors. There were cats reading books and cats curled up in drawers.

She held up a picture of a white kitten with black patches on its nose and eyebrows. "Just look at that! How could anyone possibly say no to that face?"

"They couldn't," Olivia agreed. "One look at that cuteness, and they'd say yes to anything."

Henry nodded. "Yep. Kittens are im-*paw*-sible to resist."

Suddenly, Finley felt an idea sprouting. *All I have to do is put this where Mom and Dad will see it,* she realized. *Then they'll want a kitten too! It's the purr-fect plan!*

* * *

When Finley got home, she took the magazine to her room and flipped through it. Calico kittens peeked out of flowerpots. Siamese kittens batted at yarn. Fluffy tabbies snuggled up with baby chicks. Smoky gray cats watched fish swimming in a fishbowl.

Finley was falling in love with kittens. Now all she had to do was make Mom and Dad fall in love with them too.

She thought about just handing them the magazine but figured it might be better if they discovered it for themselves. So she decided to leave it on Mom's bedside table.

That's where she keeps the books she's reading, Finley thought. *She'll reach for one and pick up an irresistible kitten instead.*

Finley slunk into her parents' bedroom and headed straight for Mom's side of the bed. She opened *Pet Perfect* to the white kitten with black eyebrows and laid it across Mom's teetering stack of books. Then she crept back down the hall to her room.

* * *

Later that night, as Finley was sitting in bed reading, Mom appeared in the doorway. "Is this yours?" she asked, holding up the *Pet Perfect* magazine.

"Yep," Finley said. "Olivia lent it to me." She pointed to the kitten on the cover. "Just look at that face. Isn't it adorable?"

Mom nodded. "It is. But you know I can't take care of —"

"Another living thing," Finley finished. "I know. *I'd* take care of it."

"You don't realize how much work it is to have a pet," Mom said.

Finley sighed. "I'll never know unless you let me try."

Mom closed the door behind her and sat on Finley's bed. She took a rabbit from the pile of stuffed animals and held it in her lap. "What's this one's name?"

"Bluebell." Finley answered. "Aunt Grace gave her to me for my fourth birthday."

"She still looks exactly the same," Mom said, turning Bluebell around. "You've taken such good care of her."

"She's just a stuffed animal," Finley said glumly. "She doesn't need much."

PET PERFECT

Mom patted Bluebell's head then looked at Finley. "It's not that we don't want you to get a pet," she said. "We know you'd do a great job. If that were the only thing to consider, we'd get one right now."

Finley frowned. "Why can't I then?"

"Most pets live a long time," Mom said. "It's a big commitment. Cats can live for up to twenty years. Chances are you'll have moved out long before then."

"I'll take it with me," Finley said. "Or I'll leave it with you so you won't be lonely when I leave."

Mom smiled. "There's still the matter of cost," she said. "Pets are expensive."

Just then there was a knock on the door, and Dad poked his head in. "Hey," he said to Finley. "Why the sad face?"

"We're talking about pets and why I can't have one."

Dad came in and stood next to Finley's bed. "We know you really want a pet. But before we'd even think about getting one, you'd need to demonstrate some responsibility. I wish we could try it out and see how it goes. But you can't take pets back."

"Too bad you can't rent them," Mom said jokingly.

Suddenly, Finley had a Fin-tastic idea. "You can't rent them, but you *can* borrow them. Maybe I could try pet sitting! When Olivia's family goes out of town, they always hire someone to take care of their pets. If I were a pet sitter, I could show some responsibility, make some money, *and* borrow someone else's pet to try it out."

Mom and Dad exchanged glances. "It's a possibility," Dad said. "We'll talk about it in the morning."

Dad gave Finley a kiss. Then Mom passed her Bluebell and tucked her in. "Goodnight," she said. "Sweet dreams."

Finley was too excited to sleep. *We'll talk about it in the morning!* she thought. *It's not a yes, but it's not a no!*

Chapter 4
READY FOR BUSINESS

The next morning, Finley woke up extra early. She got dressed and pulled her craft box out from under her bed. She grabbed a piece of thick pink paper and cut a rectangle off one of the corners.

If I'm going to be a pet sitter, she thought, *I'm going to need a business card.*

After sketching out a *Fin-tastic Pet Care* logo, with paw prints for the dots on each *i,* Finley traced her design with a fine-tipped marker. Tucking the card into her jeans pocket, she headed downstairs. Dad was in the kitchen making pancakes while Mom read the newspaper.

"We've discussed your pet-sitting idea, and we think it might be just the thing," he said. "You'll need some supervision — which Mom and I are happy to provide."

"Yes!" Finley pulled out her business card and handed it to Mom. "What do you think?"

"Fin-tastic Pet Care." Mom smiled. "I like your logo."

"I'll make more cards," Finley said. "Can we leave them in people's mailboxes? Or post some on the bulletin board at the grocery store?"

Dad shook his head. "I think we should start small. We'll spread the word to friends and neighbors. It's better to pet sit for people you know."

After breakfast, Finley created some more cards and gave Dad a stack. "Let me know when you run out," she said.

Then she got out her library books to read up on proper pet care. She was in the middle of the chapter on grooming when Mom knocked on her bedroom door.

"I have some news," Mom said.

Finley put her book down. "What kind of news?"

"Pet-sitting news. Mrs. Mullins is going out of town next week to visit her niece in New York City. Her usual pet sitter canceled, and she needs someone to take care of her cat, Goo-Goo."

Finley's eyes grew wide. "She does?"

Mom nodded. "She'll be gone for three days, but it's right next door. I'm not sure how much she'll pay you, if anything, but it would be great experience. Are you up for the job?"

"Of course I'm up for it!" Finley shrieked. "It's *purr*-fect! My first pet-sitting gig!"

"I thought that might make you happy," Mom said. "She leaves on Wednesday, so we'll have to check in with her before then and get instructions for you."

"Thanks, Mom!" Finley gave Mom a kiss on the cheek and jumped up.

"Where are you going?" Mom called after her.

"To call Henry!"

Finley bounded downstairs and grabbed the phone.

"Happy Saturday," Henry said when he answered. "What's up?"

Finley felt like she was about to explode with good news. "You'll never guess what I got!"

"A llama?"

"No — a job!"

"A job?"

"A *pet-sitting* job!"

"Wow," Henry said. "When do you start?"

"Wednesday."

"You're going to be a pro. I can't wait to hear all about it."

"Thanks," Finley said. "Today I'm going to read up on cats and make my uniform."

After she said goodbye to Henry and hung up the phone, Finley ran upstairs to grab a pencil and some fabric paints out of her craft box. Then she searched through her dresser and pulled out a plain, pink T-shirt.

"Mom!" she called from the top of the stairs, "can I paint on this old shirt?"

"Sure," Mom answered. "Just do it on the porch. And don't forget to use a drop cloth."

Finley tucked her pencil behind her ear and bounded downstairs with her T-shirt and paints. Stopping in the kitchen, she grabbed a trash bag from under the kitchen sink and headed out to the porch.

Once she'd spread out the garbage bag, Finley laid her T-shirt on top of it. Then she pulled a business card from her back pocket and sketched out a matching *Fin-tastic Pet Care* logo on the front of the shirt.

FIN-TASTIC
PET CARE

Lining up the bottles of fabric paint, Finley picked out a purplish-pink one. Then she carefully traced her letters and stood back to look.

Not bad, she thought. *I'm ready for business!*

Chapter 5
GOO-GOO

On Tuesday night, the phone rang as Finley was finishing up her homework. A few minutes later, Mom knocked on her bedroom door.

"Mrs. Mullins just called," she said. "She was wondering if you could come over so she can explain your pet-sitting duties and show you where everything is."

Finley's eyes lit up. "Definitely!"

She grabbed her jacket from the coat rack and headed for the front door.

"Whoa," Dad said as she flew through the kitchen. "Where are you off to?"

"To Mrs. Mullins' so she can show me around and tell me how to take care of Goo-Goo."

"*Goo-Goo*?" Zack made a face. "What kind of cat has a name like Goo-Goo?"

Finley shrugged. "I guess I'm about to find out."

"Have fun," Dad said. "And don't forget something to write with so you can take notes."

Finley dashed back upstairs and got her sketchbook and a pencil out of her backpack. Then she headed next door, knocked three times, and waited.

She heard a rustling inside and peered through the window in the front door. She could just make out Mrs. Mullins holding a giant black cat.

That's one big kitty, Finley thought. *It doesn't look too cuddly. And aren't black cats bad luck?*

Just then, Mrs. Mullins opened the door and flicked the porch light on. For a second, the cat's eyes flashed an eerie, glowing green.

"Hi, Finley!" Mrs. Mullins said. "Meet Geraldine — otherwise known as Goo-Goo."

Goo-Goo flattened her ears and narrowed her eyes at Finley. Her tail twitched as Mrs. Mullins held her closer.

"She hates when I mention her real name," Mrs. Mullins whispered. "It makes her cranky."

Finley reached out to pet Goo-Goo's back, and the cat gave a low, raspy growl.

"That's her way of saying hi," Mrs. Mullins said as Finley pulled her hand back. "I think she likes you." She cradled Goo-Goo in her arms. "Aw, who's my wittle bay-beee?" she cooed.

Goo-Goo growled louder and started to squirm.

"That's enough, wiggle-worm." Mrs. Mullins looked at Finley. "Better shut the door before she makes a run for it. If she ever got loose outside, she might not come back. Come on in — I'll show you where everything is."

"Okay," Finley said, stepping inside and shutting the door behind her.

"All right," Mrs. Mullins said to Goo-Goo. "Let's show Miss Finley where the treats are." But before she could bend down, Goo-Goo sprang from her arms and disappeared under the couch.

"She's being shy," Mrs. Mullins explained, "but she'll warm up to you. Come on, I'll give you a tour."

Finley flipped to a new page in her sketchbook and wrote *The Care and Keeping of Goo-Goo* at the top. Then she trailed Mrs. Mullins to the kitchen.

"Here's where I keep the cat food." Mrs. Mullins opened the cupboard under the sink and pulled out a plastic bin. "She gets one cupful a day, but sometimes I give her a teensy bit extra."

She pried the lid off the tub and scooped some food into Goo-Goo's dish. Then she pointed to a pink bowl in the corner of the room. "That's her water bowl. Just make sure it stays full."

"Got it," Finley said, writing it down.

Mrs. Mullins took out a box with a sweet-looking kitten on the front of it and shook it. "Who wants a wittle tweet?" she called in a singsong voice. "Goo-Goo! Time for tweee-eets!"

A second later, there was a flash of black, and Goo-Goo tore across the floor. Mrs. Mullins held out the treat, and Goo-Goo pounced on it. She shook it in her mouth then leaped onto one of the kitchen chairs, peering out at Finley from under the table.

"She loves those." Mrs. Mullins smiled like a proud mama. "I try not to give too many, but sometimes I just can't help it!"

Finley tried to listen carefully to Mrs. Mullins' directions, but the whole time, she felt like Goo-Goo was stalking her. She could feel those mysterious yellow-green eyes watching her every move.

Mrs. Mullins led Finley to the laundry room. "This is where I keep the kitty litter. There are garbage bags on the counter, and this is the scoop for cleaning it each day. You probably won't get near her with a brush, but here it is just in case."

She handed Finley a stiff brush full of matted, black fur. "The vet's number and my cell phone number are on the fridge in case of emergency. But you won't need them." She smiled. "I think that's about it. Any questions?"

Finley was sure there were. But her brain was so crammed full of instructions, she couldn't think of what those questions might be. So she just smiled and shook her head.

"Great!" Mrs. Mullins handed her a key chain with one silver key and a dangly charm engraved with *I ♥ CATS*. "You're all set then. I know you'll take good care of my sweet potato."

She scooped up Goo-Goo and gave her a squeeze. "Who's gonna miss her baby? That's wight, Mama is."

Goo-Goo struggled free and bolted down the hall.

Mrs. Mullins sighed as she watched her go. "I miss her already."

* * *

When Finley got home, she took out her *Pet Perfect* magazine. *Goo-Goo isn't anything like these kittens*, she thought. *But this is my first real pet-sitting job. I'll have to stick it out.*

She picked up the phone. *Maybe Henry will make me feel better. He always knows what to say.*

"So how's the pet sitting going?" Henry asked when he answered.

"Not so great," Finley said. "And I haven't even started yet. I just got back from meeting the cat. She scares me. Her eyes glow — I think she might have supernatural powers."

"All cats' eyes look like they're glowing in the right light," Henry said. "They're nocturnal, so their eyes have a reflective layer to help them see better in the dark."

"You always have an explanation for everything," Finley said.

"Knowledge is power," Henry said cheerfully. "Sometimes finding out about stuff makes it less *pet*-rifying. Plus, it's Fin-teresting."

"Ha," Finley said.

"Give the cat a chance," Henry said. "She might surprise you."

Finley sighed. "That's what I'm afraid of."

Chapter 6
SCAREDY-CAT

On Wednesday after school, Finley got ready for her first pet-sitting session. She put on her *Fin-tastic Pet Care* T-shirt and braided her hair.

Maybe I should bring Goo-Goo a present, she thought, glancing around the room.

As her eyes came to rest on the bed where Bluebell lay propped up against the pillows, an idea bloomed in Finley's brain. *I could make Goo-Goo a stuffed animal so she won't be lonely while Mrs. Mullins is away.*

Finley rooted through her dresser and pulled out an old, white sock with lace trim. Grabbing a handful of toilet paper, she stuffed the sock until it was plump. Then she got a needle and some embroidery thread from her craft box and sewed up the top, leaving some extra thread hanging for a tail. Turning the sock upside down, she drew a smiley face on the end with permanent marker.

Hello, Mousie, she thought, adding some small, rounded ears and whiskers. *That's a face any cat would love.*

Finley checked the clock. It was time to go. She cleaned up her mess and ran downstairs. "I'm headed next door!" she called into the kitchen. "I'll be back soon."

"Good luck!" Zack hollered.

"Let us know if you need help," Mom added.

"Thanks — I'll be fine!"

Finley stepped into the late-afternoon sunlight and walked across the lawn to Mrs. Mullins' house. As she got closer, she couldn't help feeling like she was being watched. Looking up at the dark house, she thought she saw a black shadow in one of the upstairs windows.

It's probably just Goo-Goo waiting for me, she thought.

A shudder ran down Finley's back as she felt around in her pocket for the key. Sliding it into the lock, she pushed the front door open and stepped inside.

"Goo-Goo?" She glanced around the room.

Finley tiptoed into the kitchen. She'd just finished refilling the food bowl when she heard a thud behind her. She spun around to see Goo-Goo, eyes gleaming, standing on the counter beside a potted plant.

"Oh, there you are," Finley said. "I've been looking all over for you."

Goo-Goo narrowed her eyes at Finley. Then she reached out a paw and nudged the plant.

"No, no," Finley said softly. "Good kitty."

Goo-Goo batted the pot again with her paw, inching it closer to the edge of the counter.

"Careful," Finley cooed, "that might —"

CRAASSH!

"— fall."

With a look of satisfaction, Goo-Goo leaped down and sauntered over to her food dish.

At least it didn't break, Finley thought as she scooped up handfuls of soil and nestled the plant back into its plastic pot.

After she'd cleaned up the mess, Finley found Goo-Goo in the living room. Spotting a feathered cat toy on a string, she grabbed it and dangled it in Goo-Goo's direction.

“Wanna play?” she asked in her most playful voice.

Goo-Goo eyed the toy warily. Finley flicked it around so it danced closer.

Goo-Goo let out a growly meow and flattened her ears. Then she swiped at the toy, sending it flying, and took another swipe at Finley’s ankles.

“Oookay,” Finley said, jumping back. “I guess you’re not in a playing kind of mood.”

Goo-Goo let out a meow that sounded like a siren’s wail.

Finley set the toy down and backed toward the door, her heart beating fast. “Well, thanks for letting me visit,” she whispered. “I think I’ll be going now.”

Once she reached the doorway, she pulled the stuffed mouse out of her pocket. “Here,” she said, “I made you something to snuggle up with.”

Goo-Goo glared as Finley set the mouse on the floor and slipped out the door.

Once she was safely outside, Finley paused to catch her breath. *Whew,* she thought. *That is one seriously cranky cat. Pet sitting Goo-Goo is going to be harder than I thought. But if I want a pet of my own, I've got to prove to Mom and Dad that I can do it.*

* * *

"What took you so long?" Zack asked as Finley breezed into the kitchen.

"Goo-Goo knocked over a plant, and I had to clean it up," Finley explained. "She swiped it off the counter. Then she growled at me."

Zack laughed. "Cats don't growl."

"This one does. I don't think she likes me."

"*I* think your imagination's getting the better of you," Zack said. "Tomorrow she'll be friendlier since she knows who you are."

Finley poured herself a glass of water. "I don't know if I can go back there alone. She kind of scares me."

"She's just a *cat,*" Zack said. "A football-sized fur ball named Goo-Goo. How scary can she possibly be?"

"More like basketball-sized," Finley corrected. "And did I mention she's a black cat? Bad luck."

"That's just a dumb superstition," Zack said. "Don't be such a *scaredy*-cat."

Finley frowned. "If you're so brave, why don't *you* go over there?"

Zack laughed. "Because *I'm* not the pet sitter."

"Seriously, why don't you come with me?" Finley said. "You could help."

Zack straightened in his chair. "As your older brother, I suppose I could provide some assistance . . . for a fee."

Finley rolled her eyes. "How much?"

"Half of what you earn."

"Will you feed her *half* of the time?" Finley asked. "Are you going to clean *half* of the litter box?"

"Ew." Zack made a face. "Not a chance. But I'll go with you so *you* can do it."

Finley glared. "That's totally unfair."

Zack shrugged. "That's business. Think about it. It's your first pet-sitting job — I know you want it to be a success."

Finley was about to walk away when an image of Goo-Goo's glowing eyes popped into her head. She didn't want to admit she needed help, but she *really* didn't want to go back alone.

"Fine," she said. "I'm not doing it for the money anyway. But you can't tell Mom and Dad why you're coming. And you can't change your mind."

"I promise." Zack crossed his heart.

Finley shook Zack's hand. "Deal."

"When do I start?" Zack asked.

"Tomorrow. Want me to make you a uniform?"

"No, thanks. I'm good." Zack grinned. "Don't worry, little sis, we'll have that furry fleabag tamed in no time."

Chapter 7

THE PET SQUAD

The next afternoon, Finley knocked on Zack's bedroom door. "Ready?"

Zack looked up from his *Invasion of the Giant Slugs* book. "For what?"

Finley rolled her eyes. "For your first day at work as a pet-sitting assistant! How could you forget?"

"Sorry," Zack said. "I was into my book. Are you sure you want me to go? I'm just getting to the good part."

Finley nodded. "I'm sure. I'll meet you at the back door. You might want to put on some long pants."

Zack put the book down. "Why?"

"Ankle protection."

"Ankle protection for what?" Evie asked as she skipped by.

"For helping with Goo-Goo," Zack said.

Evie stopped. "Can I come?" she asked in her sweetest voice. "Cats love me. My spirit animal is a kitten."

Finley shrugged. "Sure," she said. "Maybe she'll like you better than she likes me."

"Great!" Evie said. "I'll be right back. I'm going to put on my cowgirl boots!"

Once Evie and Zack were ready, the three of them headed to Mrs. Mullins' house.

"Here comes the pet squad," Zack said as Finley unlocked the door and gently pushed it open. She felt for the light switch on the wall and flicked it on.

Slipping inside, she motioned for Zack and Evie to follow. "Be careful," she warned. "Don't let her get out. She's an indoor cat."

"Let's see this terrifying piece of fluff," Zack said, closing the door behind him. "Heeeere, kitty, kitty, kitty! Dinnertime!"

"Shhhh," Finley whispered. "She doesn't like new people."

"Well, she's going to have to get over it." Zack followed Finley into the kitchen. Evie clomped along behind him. "Heeeere, kitty, kitty, kitty!" he called. "Come here, you hungry hairball!"

Finley poured cat food into Goo-Goo's bowl and filled her water dish. Then they headed back to the living room.

"Well, that wasn't so bad," Zack said. "Although we didn't even get to meet her."

"Yeah," Evie said, disappointed. "I wanted to play with her."

Just then, Finley heard a low, grumbly noise. "Listen — she's coming."

"Finally," Zack said. "I was beginning to think she was imaginary."

MMMRRRROOOOWRRR . . .

The noise grew louder.

Out of the corner of her eye, Finley saw a flicker of movement. "I think she's under there," she said, pointing to the couch.

"What's up, scaredy-cat?" Zack scooped up a fuzzy purple cat toy on a string and swung it back and forth in front of the couch.

"I wouldn't do that if I were you," Finley warned.

"Are you kidding? Cats love these things." Zack bobbed the toy up and down like a yo-yo. "Wanna play, kitty?"

Goo-Goo answered with a garbled moan.

"I'm no expert in cat language, but that did *not* sound like a happy noise," Zack said.

Just then, a paw darted out and swiped at Zack's foot.

"Easy now," Zack said, shuffling back. "Someone's a little cranky."

Goo-Goo poked her head out, hissed, and swiped again.

"Yikes!" Zack jumped. "As your older brother, I advise you to retreat," he said, edging toward the door. "Just keep calm . . . back away . . . and whatever you do, don't make any sudden —"

Just then, Zack stepped on another cat toy, which let out a piercing squeak. "Aaah!" he yelled, vaulting onto the couch.

Goo-Goo yowled and shot out from her hiding place. She skidded to a stop and twisted around to face Zack, her back arched and her eyes blazing.

"Ruuun!" Zack yelled, bolting for the door with Evie close behind.

Goo-Goo let out another wail, then vanished.

Suddenly, everything was quiet and still.

Finley looked around the room. Then she counted to ten and gathered her courage. Holding her breath, she tiptoed across the living room.

If I can just make it to the door, she thought, her heart pounding. *Almost . . . there . . .*

* * *

When Finley caught up to Zack, he was sitting on his bed reading.

"Hey," he said. "What's up?"

"What's up?" Finley repeated, her voice cracking. "You freaked out and left me with an angry cat!"

Zack shook his head. "That wasn't a cat — that was a monster. I thought she might want to play. I was only trying to help."

"That was *not* helping," Finley said. "That was *anti*-helping."

"Sorry," Zack said. "I guess you weren't exaggerating. That fanged fur ball almost clawed me." He bent down to inspect his ankle. "I'm glad I wore long pants."

Finley sank onto the bed beside him. "At least I filled her food and water bowls."

"Good thing that's over with," Zack said.

"Until tomorrow," Finley reminded him. "Don't forget, Mrs. Mullins doesn't get back for two more days."

Chapter 8
CLAW-PROOF

"You should have seen Zack's face," Finley told Henry and Olivia as she filled them in about Goo-Goo the next day at lunch. "I've never seen him run so fast."

Henry laughed. "I wish I could have been there."

"It was pretty funny," Finley said. "But seriously, what am I going to do? I have to go back there today after school."

“You could create some kind of armor,” Henry suggested.

“Like at Camp Acorn when we were scared of the vampire chipmunk,” Olivia reminded her. “I felt so much better after we made some protective gear.”

Finley laughed. “I remember.”

“I bet you could come up with some kind of claw-proof clothing,” Henry said.

“That could work,” Finley agreed. “I’ll make something when I get home and test it out tonight.”

“Good luck,” Henry told her.

“Thanks,” Finley said. “I’m going to need it.”

* * *

After school, Finley hurried home and dug around in her craft box.

I need something to wear around my ankles, she thought. *Something flexible, yet claw-proof.*

She pulled out some duct tape and Velcro patches and dashed downstairs to the kitchen. Sifting through the recycling bin, she fished out two cereal boxes.

Finley cut open one of the boxes and wrapped it around her ankle. Trimming it to fit, she covered the border with patterned duct tape. Then she stuck Velcro along the seam to keep it in place.

As she was working, Dad came in carrying a pizza box. "Dinner's ready!" he called upstairs to Zack and Evie. "Come on down!"

Finley finished making her other ankle guard and put it on. "Can you save me that box?" she asked as Dad set the pizza on the table. "I want to make something out of it."

"Sure," Dad said, sliding a slice of pizza onto Finley's plate. "We're not using it for anything."

When everyone had finished eating, Finley shook the crumbs out of the pizza box and took it up to her room. She thought about cutting the lid off, but decided against it. Instead, she duct taped it shut and started making a handle to attach to the back.

This shield will have two layers of protection, she thought, *in case Goo-Goo claws through the first one.*

As Finley was finishing the handle, Evie appeared in the doorway. "Do you think Goo-Goo used to be a sweet, little kitten like this?" she asked, holding up the *Pet Perfect* magazine and pointing to the cover.

"All cats start out as kittens," Finley told her. "Living things grow and change. We learned that in science."

Evie looked at the magazine and made a face. "I guess Goo-Goo grew and changed *a lot*."

Just then Zack peered in over Evie's shoulder. "Nice shin guards," he said, glancing at Finley's legs. "Thinking of taking up soccer?"

"For your information, these are ankle protectors," Finley said. "For pet sitting. I can make you some too."

Zack came in and took a seat on Finley's bed. "Look, I know I said I'd go with you . . . but I think you'd do better without me."

Finley put the shield down. "You are *not* going to bail on me," she said. "You promised you'd help. We even shook on it."

"I know," Zack said. "But Goo-Goo really doesn't like me. I did come up with an idea for you, though. Just dump out a humungous bowl of food and fill the sink with water. Then you won't have to keep going back."

Finley shook her head. "If that's what Mrs. Mullins had wanted, she could have put food and water out before she left instead of hiring a pet sitter. We have to go back — *all* of us. Be brave."

"What if I don't *want* to be brave?" Zack asked.

"You still have to," Finley insisted. "We had a deal. Besides, being brave doesn't mean you're not scared. It's when you're scared, and you do it anyway."

"Like when I went in the corn maze at Puckett's Pick-Your-Own Pumpkin Patch even after you told me it was haunted," Evie said. "And when I tried Finley's PB&J Pasta."

"Exactly," Finley said. She leaped up and grabbed her shield with one hand and Zack's arm with the other. "It's time for Goo-Goo vs. The Pet Squad, round two."

Zack groaned.

"Hold on." Evie ran to her room and came back wearing her soccer shin guards. "Good thinking with the shin guards," she said to Zack.

"I was kidding," Zack said. "But on second thought, it's not such a bad idea."

Chapter 9
SHREDS

Finley paused at Mrs. Mullins' front door and looked at Zack and Evie. "Ready?"

"As ready as we'll ever be," Zack said.

Finley passed him the shield and slid the key into the lock. The door creaked open, and Finley flicked on the light. Then she stopped in her tracks.

"Whoa," Evie whispered, peering over Finley's shoulder. "It snowed."

Finley stepped inside and glanced around the room. Sure enough, everything was covered in a blanket of white. She scooped up a handful of shreds from the couch and let it fall through her fingers.

"It's toilet paper," she whispered. "How many rolls do you think she used?"

"How did she even find them?" Evie asked.

"I don't know," Zack said, "but she must have some pretty sharp claws." He picked up a shred and dangled it in front of Finley's nose.

Finley surveyed the room. "How are we ever going to clean this up?"

"Better find the vacuum," Zack said. "And hope you don't find Goo-Goo with it."

Cautiously, the three of them tiptoed down the hall through the drifts of fluffy flakes. Finley opened the hall closet door and peered inside.

"Found it," she said, hauling out the vacuum and dragging it into the living room.

"I wonder what Goo-Goo will think of the noise," Evie said.

"I guess we're about to find out." Zack readied his shield. "Go ahead," he said to Finley, "I've got you covered."

Finley held her breath and turned the vacuum on. It roared and rattled as it sucked up the toilet paper snow. Zack trailed behind her, shield in one hand and a broom in the other.

After she'd finished vacuuming the hallway, Finley moved on to the living room. She checked every possible hiding place, but there was no trace of Goo-Goo. It was as if she'd disappeared.

Once the house was toilet-paper free, Finley refilled Goo-Goo's food and water bowls.

"I wonder where she is," Evie said, scanning the kitchen. "I hope she's okay."

"She must be here somewhere," Zack said. "She finished the food you left, and her water dish was half empty."

“Maybe she’s having a cat nap,” Finley said. “Henry told me that cats sleep for seventy percent of their lives.”

“Wow,” Evie said, glancing at Zack. “That’s almost as much as you.”

Zack yawned. “I’ve grown three inches this year. It’s tiring.”

As they were leaving, Finley paused outside Mrs. Mullins’ bedroom door. On the bed was Mousie, her stuffing ripped out and spread all over the pillows. But there was no sign of Goo-Goo.

So much for snuggling, Finley thought. *Poor Mousie.*

Grabbing the key from her pocket, she headed for the front door. When she got there, her heart jumped. It was wide open.

Goo-Goo isn’t sleeping, she thought. *Goo-Goo is gone!*

Just then, Zack sauntered into the living room with Evie trailing behind him.

"Who left the front door open?" Finley demanded.

Evie pointed at Zack.

"It wasn't me," Zack said.

"It was too," Evie insisted. "You were the last one in."

"Maybe the wind blew it open," Zack said. "Or maybe Goo-Goo opened it."

Finley sighed. "It doesn't matter. Come on — we have to find her. Mrs. Mullins gets back tomorrow!"

"We'll find her," Zack said. "But we have to follow my motto — Don't. Freak. Out. Bottom of the ninth, down by one run, bases loaded, at bat with two strikes? Don't freak out. Forgot your math book on the bus and you have a test? Don't freak out. Discover your fly is unzipped in the middle of reciting your English poem? Don't freak out."

Finley turned and met Zack's eyes. "If Goo-Goo is gone, I'm freaking out."

"It won't help," Zack said. "Besides, we don't even know that she's lost. She's probably watching us right now, planning her next sneak attack."

Evie walked to the window and peered out. "What if she ran away?"

"She was a miserable cat," Zack said. "We could replace her with one that looks the same but acts nicer."

"Mrs. Mullins loves her just the way she is," Finley said. "She would definitely notice the difference. And she is *definitely* going to freak out."

"Fine," Zack said. "Heere, kitty, kitty! Heeeere, kitty-kitty-kitty!"

Finley covered her ears. "Ugh. Stop. If she hasn't run away already, she will now."

Zack shrugged. "Just trying to help."

"Wait," Finley said. "I remember what makes her come."

She stood and put her hands around her mouth. "Who wants a wittle tweet?" she called, trying to mimic Mrs. Mullins' singsong voice. "Goo-Goo! Time for tweee-eets!"

"Tweets?" Zack raised an eyebrow.

"Don't look at me like that. Mrs. Mullins has a special way of talking to Goo-Goo," Finley explained.

"Whatever you say," Zack replied.

The three took turns calling until their voices were hoarse, but Goo-Goo didn't come.

Zack glanced at his watch. "We'd better go or Mom and Dad will wonder why we're taking so long."

"Let's go home and try again after dessert," Evie suggested. "Maybe she'll come out of hiding if we leave. Or maybe at least her food will be eaten, and we'll know she's still around someplace."

"That's not a bad idea," Finley said. "It's worth a try."

"Remember, she's not missing until we know she's not here," Zack said, looking at Evie. "We don't need to tell Mom and Dad — yet."

"Right." Evie pretended to lock her lips and throw away the key.

Finley frowned. *If Goo-Goo is gone, we'll have to tell them sooner or later. And my chances of having a pet will be gone too.*

Chapter 10

NO LITTERING

"Dessert is served," Dad announced as Finley, Zack, and Evie burst through the door. He set three thick pieces of chocolate cake on the kitchen table. "By the way, how's the cat sitting going?"

"Great!" Finley, Zack, and Evie said all together.

Finley washed her hands and sat at the table.

"So what kind of stuff does Goo-Goo do?" Mom asked.

"Cat stuff." Finley took a big bite of her cake, hoping Mom and Dad would lay off the questions if her mouth was full.

"What did *you* do today?" Zack asked Mom, changing the subject. "How was work?"

"It was good," Mom said. "I finished up a big project. We restored an old firehouse downtown. The owners are going to live there."

"I wish we could live in an old firehouse," Evie said. "I'd slide down the fire pole every morning and jump right into the car. Then we'd never be late for school."

"Speaking of school, I'm going to get a head start on homework." Zack finished off his cake and pushed his chair away from the table. He caught Finley's eye as he took his plate to the counter.

"Me too," Finley said, jumping up. "Thanks for dessert."

Zack was waiting for her in the hall. "Let's go next door," he said.

"We're headed to do one last check on Goo-Goo!" Finley yelled into the kitchen.

"You're taking such good care of her," Mom said. "Don't be long — it looks like it's going to rain."

"Wait for me!" Evie hollered, running to get her rain jacket.

"Hurry up," Zack called. "It's starting to pour."

Finley grabbed an umbrella, and they trudged over to Mrs. Mullins' porch. Opening the front door, they crept in like ninjas.

"This time I'm locking it from the inside," Finley said, turning the key in the lock and slipping it into the front pocket of her jeans. "Then there's no way it can *blow open*."

As Finley turned around, she caught a whiff of something awful.

"Whew!" Zack said, fanning his face. "Have you cleaned the litter box lately?"

"Whoops." Finley grimaced. "I kind of forgot."

"I think it's time," Zack said, holding his nose.

Finley crept down the hall and into the laundry room. "That's funny," she said. "It doesn't smell nearly as bad in here."

"Maybe we're just getting used to it," Evie suggested.

Finley got a garbage bag, held her breath, and changed the litter. Then she threw the bag into one of the trash cans in the garage.

"There," she said. "Better late than never."

"Something in this house *still* stinks," Zack said as they stepped into the hall.

"Let's sniff it out," Evie suggested.

Zack shuddered. "Gross."

"You two go that way, and I'll go this way," Finley instructed as she headed for the kitchen.

Peeping through the doorway, she tiptoed silently across the tile floor. She peeked under chairs. She looked in every cupboard. She checked every drawer.

Nothing.

As Finley slunk back down the hall toward the living room, the stench got stronger.

"I think I'm getting closer," she called over the drumming rain. Suddenly, lightning flashed, and she spotted Zack frozen in the bathroom doorway.

"I found it," he whispered, holding his nose, "and it's not pretty."

Finley buried her face in her sleeve and peered over Zack's shoulder into the tub. Her stomach heaved. "If she didn't want to go in the litter, she could have at least used the toilet."

"She needs a kitty diaper," Evie said, squeezing in next to Finley.

"Come on," Zack said, "I can't stand here any more."

"On the bright side, at least she didn't run away," Finley said, trying to sound cheerful.

"I don't know if that's the bright side," Zack said. "You'd better get the scoop. I'll get a garbage bag and something to clean up this mess."

"I'll keep watch at the bathroom door in case of a surprise attack," Evie said.

Zack rummaged in the hall closet. He came back with a roll of paper towels, some bathroom cleaner, a trash bag, rubber gloves, and a scrub brush.

"I'm starting to think that having a pet might actually increase my stress level," Zack said as he and Finley cleaned up the mess and scrubbed the tub. "Especially one like Goo-Goo."

"At least Mrs. Mullins gets back tomorrow," Finley said. "We've got to find Goo-Goo and make sure she's still here."

Zack pointed to the tub. "Wasn't that enough proof?"

"She could have done that before she ran away," Finley said. "I want to see her with my own two eyes."

Zack put away the cleaning stuff, and Finley took the trash out.

"She's got to be here somewhere," Zack said.

"This house has too many hiding places," Finley said. "We should split up and search it from top to bottom."

Just then, thunder crashed. Finley's heart jumped.

"I've got the downstairs," Zack volunteered.

"I'll search the upstairs bedrooms," Finley said. "Evie, you keep a lookout — and yell if you see anything suspicious."

Chapter 11

HERE, KITTY, KITTY

Finley crept up the stairs, trying not to make a sound. When she got to the top, she stopped to listen. The only noise was the tapping of rain on the roof.

She padded into the first bedroom and flicked on the light. She checked behind the door and under the bed. Nothing but dust bunnies and an old sock. She opened the closet door and swished the clothes around.

Nothing.

One down and one to go, Finley thought.

Just then she heard a scraping sound, like claws on a mirror.

SCREEAK, SCREEAK, SCREEAK.

She tiptoed across the hall to the second bedroom.

SCREEAK, SCREEAK, SCREEAK.

Finley pushed the door open.

SCREEAK, SCREEAK.

The noise was coming from outside. It sounded like claws scratching on the window.

"Goo-Goo?" Finley's heart beat fast as she tiptoed closer and threw open the curtains.

The wind howled as a tree branch scraped against the windowpane. Finley breathed a sigh of relief and snapped the curtains shut.

Just then, lightning flashed. A clap of thunder rattled the windows, and the lights went out. As Finley stood there in the dark, she heard a low, moaning noise.

MMMRRRROOOOWRRR . . .

“Zack!” she whisper-called.

There was no answer.

Finley felt her way down the stairs and along the hall toward the front door. She was almost to the kitchen when she bumped into Evie.

“Aaah!” Evie yelped as Finley plowed into her back.

“Sorry,” Finley whispered. “I can’t see a thing.”

“I saw a flashlight in here earlier,” Zack said, rifling through the hall closet. “Yes — found it!”

MMMRRRROOOOWRRR . . .

“Listen,” Zack whispered. “She’s back.” He turned the flashlight on, and a circle of light illuminated the floor.

"Where is she?" Finley asked. "I hope she's okay."

"Maybe she's stuck in a cupboard," Zack suggested.

"There's only one way to find out." Finley slunk into the kitchen and readied her shield. "Shine the light in this direction. One, two, three . . ."

Zack shone the flashlight beam on the cupboard doors, and Finley flung them open, one by one.

"Just pots and pans," she announced, peering inside.

"Try that one," Zack said shining the flashlight on the cupboard below the sink.

"Stand back," Finley said. She threw the doors open. "Cat food . . . dish soap . . . sponges . . ."

MMMRRRROOOOWRRR . . .

The moaning started up again, like a car motor revving.

"It's definitely getting louder," Finley said, opening another cupboard door.

"Finley," Evie whispered.

"Hold on, just two more . . ."

"Finley," Zack croaked.

Finley sat back on her heels. "What?"

Zack pointed up. The shadow of a giant cat loomed above them.

MMMRRRROOOOWRRR . . .

Goo-Goo perched on top of the cabinets, looking down on the kitchen like a queen surveying her land. Her eyes glowed alien-green in the flashlight beam.

"Now I know how a mouse feels," Finley whispered.

Goo-Goo's eyes narrowed. Her tail twitched. She crouched like a lion about to pounce on her prey.

One . . . two . . . three . . . four . . . Finley counted the seconds. Her heart pounded in her ears.

Stay calm, she told herself. *She can sense your fear. Five . . . six . . . seven . . .*

MMMRRRROOOOWRRR . . .

Finley tried to slow her breathing. *In through the nose . . . out through the mouth. . . . Or is it the other way around?*

"Retreat," Zack whispered. He nodded his head toward the kitchen door, keeping the flashlight beam trained on Goo-Goo.

Finley put one foot behind the other and started to back away. Zack and Evie followed. They were almost to the doorway when Goo-Goo let out a garbled wail. She sprang off the ledge and sailed through the air, landing on the kitchen table with a thud.

Finley spun around and sprinted for the front door with Evie on her heels. Shadows danced across the walls and ceiling as Zack tore after them, flashlight bobbing in his hand.

"Hurry!" he cried as Finley reached the door. "Open it!"

Finley slid to a stop and felt around in her front pocket. The only thing there was a hole. "I can't!" she yelled. "The key's gone!"

Chapter 12
LUCKY

"What do you mean the key is gone?" Zack cried.

Finley scanned the floor. "It must have fallen out of my pocket."

Zack tugged on the doorknob with both hands. "We're locked in!"

Clink! Clink! Clink!

Zack froze, and Finley looked up to see Goo-Goo batting something silver across the floor.

"Uh-oh," she whispered. "I think she found it."

Just then, Goo-Goo swiped the key and sent it skittering into Finley's feet. But before Finley could bend down to pick it up, Goo-Goo pounced on it and batted it away.

"I think she's trying to play," Evie said.

"She knows we want it, and she's not going to give it up," Zack whispered. "We'll be stuck here forever like some creepy movie."

Finley turned to Zack. "Don't. Freak. Out."

Goo-Goo dribbled the key from one end of the living room to the other, watching them with her yellow-green eyes. Then she wound up and flung it under the couch.

"Nice slapshot," Zack muttered. "She should play hockey."

Finley slid her hands into her back pockets. Her fingers closed around something round and smooth. She pulled it out and held it in her palm. Her lucky rock.

Whoops, Finley thought, glancing at Evie. *I guess I never put it in my backpack. And Evie didn't take it after all.*

Suddenly, Finley had an idea. Rubbing her thumb against the rock, she made a silent wish. She waited until Goo-Goo had fished the key out and dribbled it a bit closer. Then she flicked the rock across the floor.

Goo-Goo's ears perked up. She glanced at Finley, then scampered after it.

Finley tiptoed toward the key, but before she could grab it, Goo-Goo was back with the rock. She sat there, looking smug as she stared up at Finley with her two prizes.

Finley's heart sank. *So much for my escape plan,* she thought.

"Don't move," Evie whispered.

Goo-Goo nudged the rock closer and brushed up against Finley's leg. Finley held her breath and tried not to move a muscle. Then she heard a warm, rumbly sound.

"I think she's *purring*," Zack said.

Just then the lights came back on.

Goo-Goo circled around Finley's legs and head-butted Zack's ankle, purring louder.

"If I weren't so terrified, I'd laugh," Zack said. "Aaah! That tickles!"

"I read in one of my pet books that cats brush against you to mark their territory," Finley said.

"So now I'm *hers*?" Zack rolled his eyes.

Goo-Goo looped through Finley's legs once more, rubbed her side against Evie, then plodded away toward the kitchen, leaving the rock and key at Finley's feet. As soon as the cat's tail had rounded the corner out of sight, Finley slowly bent down to pick the objects up. "I think she might actually *like* us," she said.

"Let's go," Zack said, "before she changes her mind."

Once they were safely outside, Finley locked the door behind them. "We did it," she said, giving Zack and Evie high fives. "Thanks to my lucky rock."

"Where did you find it?" Evie said. "I thought I'd lost it."

"That must have been a different rock you lost." Finley smiled sheepishly. "It was in my pocket all along. Sorry I blamed you for taking it."

"I'm happy you found it," Evie said. "Just in time to save the day."

* * *

The next afternoon, the doorbell rang. Finley peeked through the window and saw Mrs. Mullins standing on the porch with Goo-Goo in her arms.

"I'm back!" she announced when Finley opened the door. "I've come to thank you and pick up my key."

"How was your trip?" Finley asked.

"Fantastic!" Mrs. Mullins said, beaming. "And I didn't worry once since I knew Goo-Goo was in such good hands." She patted Goo-Goo's head gently. "I hope you weren't too much trouble, sugar-paws. Sometimes you can be quite a character."

"She's got a lot of personality," Finley agreed, picking up the key from the hall table and handing it back. "I think she warmed up to me, just like you said."

"Well, thank you again," Mrs. Mullins said. "This is for you." She handed Finley an envelope. Then she grabbed Goo-Goo's paw and made her wave at Finley. "Bye-bye, Finwey! Thanks for taking care of me!"

Goo-Goo flattened her ears and pulled her paw away as Mrs. Mullins turned to go.

"Bye, Goo-Goo," Finley said with a wave.

Goo-Goo stared at Finley with her yellow-green eyes, then gave her a slow wink.

Finley closed the door and headed down the hall to the kitchen. Zack was reading at the table.

Carefully opening the envelope, Finley slid out a thank-you card with a cat on the front. There were several crisp bills inside. "Thirty bucks! I didn't even know I was getting paid."

Zack looked up from his book. "You didn't? What were you going to pay me — half of nothing?"

Finley smiled and shrugged. "Here you go." She handed Zack his share.

"That's the hardest-earned money I've ever made," Zack said. "I don't think I'm ever going to spend it."

Just then, Evie came bounding into the room. "What's up?"

Zack looked at Finley, then handed a five-dollar bill to Evie. Finley did the same.

"Wow!" Evie said. "What's that for?"

"Helping with Goo-Goo," Finley said. "You worked as hard as we did."

"Way to go, Fin," Dad said, breezing by on his way outside. "Mrs. Mullins seemed really happy with the job you did. That was a lot of work."

You have no idea, Finley thought, glancing at Zack. He grinned like he'd read her mind.

"So," Zack said after Dad had left, "we survived Goo-Goo."

"Barely," Finley said. "My first pet-sitting gig was almost a disaster."

"More like a *cat*-astrophe." Zack laughed.

"I'm sure your next job will be much easier," Evie said. "But in the meantime, maybe you could ask for a hermit crab."

Finley shook her head. "I'm still holding out for a llama one day. But for now, I've got a better idea." She reached into her pocket and pulled out her lucky rock. "Meet Roxie, my pet rock," she said, handing the rock to Evie. "She likes to be held."

"How can you tell she's a she?" Evie asked, turning the rock over in her hand.

Finley laughed. "I just can."

"Does she have claws?" Zack asked.

Finley shook her head. "No claws. Plus, she doesn't make a mess. She's a great listener. And she doesn't need food, water, or a litter box."

Zack patted the rock with one finger. "Sounds like the perfect pet to me."

"Maybe one day I'll get a real pet," Finley said. "But at the moment, I'll stick with Roxie."

"Are you still in the pet-sitting business?" Evie asked.

Finley nodded. "After pet sitting Goo-Goo, I'm ready for anything." She looked at Zack and Evie. "What about you? I could use some help."

Zack frowned. “I thought you said I was *anti*-help.”

“I did.” Finley smiled. “But I was wrong. The three of us make a good pet squad. We might not always get along, but when we work together, we make a pretty Fin-tastic team.”

About the Author

Jessica Young grew up in Ontario, Canada. The same things make her happy now as when she was a kid: dancing, painting, music, digging in the dirt, picnics, reading, and writing. Like Finley Flowers, Jessica loves making stuff. When she was little, she wanted to be a tap-dancing flight attendant/veterinarian, but she's changed her mind! Jessica currently lives with her family in Nashville, Tennessee.

About the Illustrator

When Jessica Secheret was young, she had strange friends that were always with her: felt pens, colored pencils, brushes, and paint. After Jessica repainted all the walls in her house, her parents decided it was time for her to express her "talent" at an art school — the famous École Boulle in Paris. After several years at various architecture agencies, Jessica decided to give up squares, rulers, and compasses and dedicate her heart and soul to what she'd always loved — putting her own imagination on paper. Today, Jessica spends her time in her Paris studio, drawing for magazines and children's books in France and abroad.

Make Your Own Pet Rock

Make your own pet, just like Finley — no house training or grooming required! Get creative and combine your favorite pet features into your pet rock! Make sure to have an adult supervise when using paint or paint markers.

What You'll Need:

- one rock that fits just right in your hand
- marker
- non-toxic paint markers or non-toxic acrylic paint and a fine-tipped paintbrush — add a bowl of water and paper towels if using this option
- googly eyes and white glue (optional)

What to Do:

1. Think of different animal features (like tail, ears, wings, and fins) and use a marker to sketch them on your rock. Combine features from different animals to create your Fin-tastic pet! (Try sketching them on paper first to find the combination of features you like best.)
2. Using a fine-tipped paintbrush and acrylic paint or paint markers, color in and outline your pet's features.
3. Glue on googly eyes, using just a dot of glue on each one. (This step — and eyes — can be optional.)
4. Think of a name for your pet and prepare a special spot for it in your room.

Personal logo

If you had a business card or T-shirt, what would it look like? Design a personal logo — a symbol that stands for you. Be sure to include your name and favorite colors!

What You'll Need:

- white paper or sketchbook
- pencil, eraser, and markers or colored pencils

What to Do:

1. Think about who you are and what you like to do. What object or animal could you choose to represent yourself? What are your favorite colors? If you had a business, what would it be?

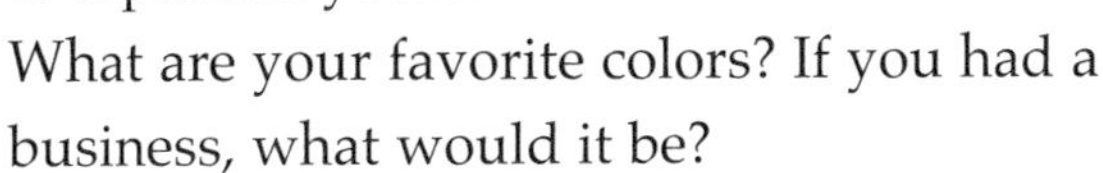

2. Write your name or your initials on a piece of paper. Try using different types of letters — lowercase or capital, straight or curvy, stick letters or bubble letters. Are there parts of your letters that could be changed into a visual symbol, like the paw print Finley used to dot the *i* in her name? Or maybe your name could be inside or on top of a symbol.
3. Sketch out some designs using your ideas. Then pick your favorite and outline it and color it in to make your own Fin-tastic logo!

Be sure to check out all of Finley's creative, Fin-tastic adventures!

Finley Flowers
Super Spooktacular
by
Jessica Young

Finley Flowers
by
Jessica Young
New & Improved

Finley Flowers
Room to Bloom
by
Jessica Young

Finley Flowers
Fin-Tastic Fashion
by
Jessica Young